SO-CIE-656

ZACHARY
in
The Winner

by Bertrand Gauthier
illustrations by Daniel Sylvestre

For a free color catalog describing Gareth Stevens's list of high-quality books, call 1-800-341-3569 (USA) or 1-800-461-9120 (Canada).

Library of Congress Cataloging-in-Publication Data

Gauthier, Bertrand, 1945-
    [Zunik dans le chouchou. English]
    Zachary in The winner / text by Bertrand Gauthier ; illustrated by Daniel Sylvestre.
       p. cm. — (Just me and my dad)
    Summary: Zachary doesn't understand why his dad always lets Zachary's friend Andrea Abbott have her way.
    ISBN 0-8368-1009-0
    [1. Fathers and sons—Fiction. 2. Winning and losing—Fiction. 3. Friendship—Fiction.] I. Sylvestre, Daniel, ill. II. Title. III. Title: Winner. IV. Series.
PZ7.G2343Zag 1993
[E]—dc20
                                      93-7718

This edition first published in 1993 by
Gareth Stevens Publishing
1555 North RiverCenter Drive, Suite 201
Milwaukee, Wisconsin 53212, USA

This edition first published in 1993 by Gareth Stevens, Inc. Original edition published in 1987 by Les éditions la courte échelle inc., Montréal, under the title *Zunik dans le chouchou.* Text © 1987 by Bertrand Gauthier. Illustrations © 1987 by Daniel Sylvestre.

Series editor: Patricia Lantier-Sampon
Series designer: Karen Knutson

Printed in the United States of America
1 2 3 4 5 6 7 8 9 9 97 96 95 94 93

At this time, Gareth Stevens, Inc., does not use 100 percent recycled paper, although the paper used in our books does contain about 30 percent recycled fiber. This decision was made after a careful study of current recycling procedures revealed their dubious environmental benefits. We will continue to explore recycling options.

Gareth Stevens Publishing
MILWAUKEE

There's Andrea Abbott, Helen's daughter.
Helen is my father's friend.

Today, my father and I are looking after
Andrea while her mother is out shopping.

Of course, she went to tell my father.
She always does that.

When Andrea Abbott is there, my father always takes her side. He blames me for everything. She's going to win again, like the other day at the skating rink.

Andrea and I went skating. There were lots of people at the rink, and we were having fun.

Then Andrea asked my father to pull her. I wanted him to hold my hand, too. I told him, but he didn't pay any attention. He said it was Andrea's turn.

3 1833 03889 0429

My father went
around the rink
four times with her
and only three times
with me. I know;
I was counting.

11

Then, when we were driving home in the car, Andrea wanted to sit in the front with my father. He let her. He always lets her do everything she wants. She won again.

Sometimes, I think my father forgets that he's my father and not Andrea Abbott's.

It's my turn to win, I thought. I like
playing double dice, and when I play
with my father, I do really well.

I can't wait until her mother comes.
Good riddance! My friend Marlene is a
lot more fun.

I hate it when my father likes Andrea Abbott more than me.